Night Before the
The Night Before
Christmas

To many happy Christmas memories,
however crazy some may seem—N.W.

To Satchmo: A good dog—M.L.

ISBN-13: 978-0-545-05201-6
ISBN-10: 0-545-05201-7

12 11 10 9   10 11 12/0

Printed in the U.S.A.   40

First Scholastic printing, December 2007

Night Before the
The ˬNight Before
Christmas

By Natasha Wing
Illustrated by Mike Lester

SCHOLASTIC INC.
New York Toronto London Auckland Sydney
Mexico City New Delhi Hong Kong Buenos Aires

'Twas the night before the night before Christmas,
with too much to do.
Our tree wasn't up yet,
and Mom had the flu.

Our cookies were burned.
There were presents to wrap.
Mom sniffled, "What I need
is a long winter's nap."

But instead we drove miles
to go get our tree.
Last week there were millions,
now there were three.

Dad tied the tree to our car.
"This will just have to do."
Mom nodded glumly
and sneezed, "Ah–ah–ACHOO!"

We dragged in our tree
through the front door.
It dropped half its needles
all over the floor.

Just then, Patrick pointed
to something quite shocking.
Oh, no! There were holes
in everyone's stocking!

Instead we hung socks
by the chimney with care.
I hoped that Saint Nick
would fill up my spare.

Things will get better, I thought, as I crawled into bed.
Maybe visions of sugarplums will dance in my head.
Instead, I lay wondering, gazing up at the moon.
What on earth is a sugarplum? Is it a candy or a prune?

Early the next morning, I woke up from a dream.
"Be careful, Harold!" I heard my mom scream.
Out on the lawn, there arose such a clatter,
I sprang from my bed to see Dad on a ladder.

He was stringing up lights
on the rooftop and gutters,
outlining the railings,
the windows and shutters.

When he plugged in the cord,
not a single light lit.
Did we have extra bulbs?
Yes...but none of them fit.

So off to the mall
our family did drive.
When Dad saw the crowds
he gasped, "Sakes alive!"

We searched every store.
All the lights were sold out.
But I found something for Grandpa—
Silly Gilly the Trout.

Finally all done
with our last-minute shopping,
we flew past the food court
without even stopping.

"But I want to see Santa,"
Patrick said with a whine.
We pushed through the crowd—
Wow! What a line!

It wrapped 'round the counters
and down the first floor,
then wound through Kids Clothing
and out the front door.

After waiting for hours—
At last! Our big chance!
Santa roared, "Ho! Ho! Ho!"
Then Pat wet his pants.

So on the way home,
we sang the Jingle bell song,
all the while I was thinking
nothing else could go wrong.

When what to our wondering
eyes should appear,
but a gigantic mess,
that much was clear.

The tree was knocked over!
My snow globe was shattered.
Ornaments were broken.
Tinsel was scattered.

"Bad kitty!" I shouted,
then Mom started to weep.
"Christmas is ruined.
And I need some sleep!"

"No, it's not, sugarplum,
These things are just stuff.
Christmas is about love.
And we have quite enough."

He tucked Mom in bed
for some much-needed rest.
Then we three busy elves
all gave it our best.

As snow gently fell, turning the earth sparkly white,
I knew in my heart Christmas would turn out just right.
Dad read us a book and gave us a kiss.
It was my favorite story, and it began like this...

*'Twas the night before Christmas,
when all through the house
Not a creature was stirring,
not even a mouse.*